TANTE FRAN'S
MAY 68 BOOK CLUB

Tante Fran's May 68 Book Club

choose your own revolution

BLAIRE SQUISCOLL

First published by Kabuff Books in 2025

This choose your own revolution novel is entirely a work of fiction. The names, characters and incidents portrayed in it are the work of the author's imagination. Any resemblance to actual persons, living or dead, events or localities is entirely coincidental.
Blaire Squiscoll asserts the moral right to be identified as the author of this work.
First edition
ISBN: 978-1-9993676-2-6

For that shoe shop we liked in Frankfurt

CONTENTS

~~

La Méthode

68

~~

L'Odéon

75

~~

Sorbonne

78

~~

Big Riot

85

~~

Père Lachaise

90

~~

Hachis Parmentier

94

~~

L'Écrivain

~~

L'Éditeur

PROLOGUE

Ding-a-ling!

Normally, Fran loved the cheery sound of the bell above her shoe shop door. It was a friendly companion over the course of her day, merrily punctuating the time she spent chatting with the shoppers of Frankfurt and watching her small business thrive. Ding-a-ling ch-ching!

Even better, sometimes the jovial bell rang as her friends arrived for the weekly Book Club she held out the back of the shop, amongst the shelves of twentieth-century classics and the slogan-painting materials. A bit of book talk, wine drinking, knitting, and rebellious chat was the perfect way to break up the week, if you asked Fran.

Today, though, she barely noticed the bell. Her mind was whirring.

The customer had barely spoken, but with those blue eyes and that dark hair she was the spitting image of her mother — a ghost from the past. Fran had been expecting her, sure, but the sight was still a shock. It wasn't every day you encountered the daughter of a friend you'd said goodbye to decades ago.

Then Fran's nephew, the burly policeman Caspian, had swung by and the two young people had gone off together. Hot on the heels of who knew what at the Frankfurter Buchmesse — something that sounded dangerous, something that sounded political.

Something that sounded a lot like scenes Fran had encountered before.

She'd encountered them with Beatrice's mother Charmian. Ah, the old gang: Fran, Charmian, Sylva and DeNanielle. Fran's eyes misted over. Sitting on the stool behind the counter of her shoe shop, she let her mind travel back, back, back in time, to when they all met. Back to May 68.

To Paris.

The European springtime of history.

The city of love, revolution ... and reading.

Hurry up! The train for Paris is leaving ... Go to page 4.

THE 11.11 FROM
FRANKFURT

Fran heaved her leather suitcase onto the train, regretting for a moment the number of books she'd packed alongside her shoes. She caught her breath, reading the destination sign in the carriage window.

FRANKFURT-KÖLN-BRUXELLES-PARIS.

Paris.

A smile spread across her face. The city of Balzac, Bourdieu, de Beauvoir and Bernstein. She picked up her case with renewed energy, and after checking her ticket for the 100th time, found her seat.

'Fräulein, your suitcase - can I help you?'

She looked up to see the lazy smile of a train inspector, his muscled arm pointing at the rope luggage holder above her head.

She hesitated, briefly questioning her re-solve for emancipation from social roles, then grinned and shook her head, her newly cropped hair springing around her face. She swung her bag upwards, and dropped into her seat. The inspector moved down the carriage, shrugging.

A whistle sounded, the train juddered, and the platform started to move outside of the window. The journey had begun.

***

Fran frowned at the words on the well-worn letter in front of her, her fingers drumming lightly on its soft paper. She was still convinced the plan to meet up was too vague. Fran had never met her Australian pen pal before, but Charmian's personality shone through in letters: sanguine confidence and a loose relation to what Fran called reality - dates, places, times, seasons. Had Charmian even received Fran's carefully written note with the details of her arrival at the Gare du Nord?

Her brow furrowed, suddenly questioning her escapade. She tapped the envelope on the table, her eye travelling down the carriage. A slim female figure stepped out from the toilet compartment, and cast her eye rapidly up and down. She met Fran's watching blue eyes, marched up the aisle and indicated the free seat next to her. Without waiting for a reply, she blithely plonked herself down after jamming her burgundy suede tote next to Fran's bag.

'Sylva,' she said in heavily accented German. 'Has he gone?'

'I'm Fran,' Fran said, reaching out to shake the hand proffered to her. 'Who are you talking about?'

'Lover-boy ticket inspector,' Sylva replied.

Fran looked behind her. 'Erm, yes ... ?'

Sylva smiled, and settled down further into the seat, smoothing down her brightly patterned mini skirt. 'Good!' She tapped the side of her nose. 'I'm travelling *sans-billet*, as they call it at our destination.'

Fran looked in shock at her new companion. 'No ticket? Where have you come from?'

'Don't be so bourgeois!' Sylva laughed. 'Revolutionaries demand passage! I come direct from Praha.' She shot a look at Fran, her dark eyes burning bright. 'You have heard what is happening in my country?'

Fran thought of the front-page headlines she'd seen of the recent protests, 500 km east of her Frankfurt home. She'd followed the reports avidly, and here right by her side was a real revolutionary!

'Of course,' she replied. 'Tell me about it, it sounds so important!'

'Oh, it is,' Sylva responded. 'Since March, there have been constant gatherings of people in Na příkopech park, under the statue of St Wenceslas in Wenceslas Square, talking about the past and present without fear. All our radio and television broadcasts are full of debates and different ideas. No censorship! Enough to make any Czechoslovak woman smile ... '

The two young women continued their excited chatter as the train wound its way west across Europe, barely noticing the first stop at Köln. Sylva described in thrilling detail the scenes in Praha and the atmosphere on the streets: freedom of speech, decentralisation of administration, loosening of restrictions on movement, and also, as Sylva told her in a loud whisper, free love!

Fran giggled, and looked round the carriage to see if anyone had heard. All the other passengers continued their quiet conversations or snored into their newspapers.

'And now, I'm travelling to Paris to meet with the students there,' Sylva concluded. 'To talk about the new philosophies and actions. Perhaps to fall madly in love with an intensely charismatic French philosopher in a beret ... Paris, the city of philosophy, freedom and filet mignon!' She smiled, and pinched Fran's arm. 'And you, Fräulein Fran, what's your plan?'

Fran fingered her envelope again, her plan suddenly seeming a little pedestrian compared to Sylva's heady talk of revolution.

'I ... I'm meeting a friend, from Australia. We're pen pals.' She hesitated, unsure if her radical new friend would share her and Charmian's interests in books and the postal system. 'We write letters discussing our latest good reads. It's a great way to find out about the tastes of a reader from another part of the world.'

'I love reading!' said Sylva, smiling broadly, pulling a battered volume out of her bag. 'Ah, if only some of our latest poets were already translated into your language, you would love them, I know it.' She began to declaim rapidly to the passing countryside, her brows accentuating the rhyme at the end of each line.

Fran leafed rapidly through her European Multilingual Phrasebook (she always marvelled at how many different languages it contained for its modest size, barely larger than her palm). 'Is that about a meeting by a river under the moon between a man and a woman, and the tensions arising from the mutually ir-reconcilable demands of desire, justice, family and tradition?' she asked.

'Yes!' replied Sylva, astonished. 'How did you know?'

Fran smiled. 'Just a guess. Look! We're nearly there! There's the Eiffel Tower ... Paris at last!'

They both threw themselves at the window as the train rolled into the Gare du Nord.

Roll into the Gare du Nord! Go to page 12.

GARE DU NORD

Few people who have been to Gare du Nord have failed to notice its grandeur. You may be sure that Fran did not. 'I know it interrupts our momentum,' she confessed to Sylva with a shy smile, 'but I simply must consult my Wee Kit-Pedia to learn more about this place.'

'Your what?' Sylva queried, with another lift of her expressive brows.

Fran reached into her leather suitcase and pulled out a book. 'This encyclopedia is sourced from crowd wisdom. It is an entirely new publishing model,' she said, flicking through to find the page on Gare du Nord. 'Ah, there we have it.'

'Gare du Nord, Station of the North! One of the six large terminus stations of the mainline network of Paris, France. By the year 2019, it is estimated that this station will serve 222 million passengers per year, making it the busiest railway station in Europe by total passenger numbers! Built between 1861 and 1864, the edifice was designed by the French architect Jacques Hittorff. And who was Jacques Hittorff?' said Fran, flicking to another page, 'A former inspector of construction sites; a designer of cast iron and glass domes; an observer of Sicily; a lover of colour.'

'Oh! Ye former home of the chemin de fer du nord, ye terminus and origin and waystation, ye site of platforms 1-36 numbered left to right. Three cheers for the Gare du Nord!'

'Fran?! Is it you?' A cheerful voice interrupted Fran's musings on their grand destination, meaning she never found out that its giant iron support pillars had been made in a Glasgow foundry, the only place large enough in the whole of Europe for the task. But after all, this isn't an engineering manual.

In front of Fran, excitedly waving, was a figure she had only seen before in a blurry black and white photograph. Deep blue eyes, glossy black hair, and a smile that lit up her whole face.

'Charmian? You got my letter, then?' Fran switched to English, as Charmian shrugged, then reached out to hug her pen pal.

'Fran, here we are at last. Paris! I read so many books on the plane on the way from Australia, I can't wait to tell you about them all. It'll be so much quicker than by letter! Who is this?' Charmian said interrupting her own flow of words, and indicating to Sylva.

'Sylva Cernik,' replied Sylva, holding out her hand formally, which Charmian shook. 'From Praha. I met Fran on the train. In fact our adventures have already begun. Where to next?'

Charmian nodded, and smiled at Fran. 'A Book Club recruit, Fran?'

'Yes, she likes poetry. And she was telling me about this new novel from her country, called *The Joke*.'

Sylva broke in. 'It's about communist totalitarianism, everyone in Praha is reading it.'

'Sounds hilarious,' replied Charmian. 'Look, I've found us somewhere to stay, in the Quartier Latin. It's where all the students are. They were advertising some spare rooms on a message board. Do you want to join us Sylva?'

'Sure! I haven't arranged anything yet.'

Fran looked between her two friends, one new, one now fully embodied. Her smile broadened. 'To the Metro!'

Do you want to head immediately to the Latin Quarter? Go to page 20.

Or would you like to find out more about the engineering of the Gare du Nord? (maybe this *is* an engineering manual). Go to page 17.

ENGINEERING MANUAL: GARE DU NORD

So, you'd like to read an engineering manual instead of or as well as your other reading material? You've come to the right place.

Engineering is equal parts magic and science. Science is equal parts imagination and formulae. Formulae consist of symbols, which are tools of the imagination, literally describing something that they are not. Yet these tools of the imagination adhere to rules that mean real things (like towers and aeroplanes) stay up.

The Gare du Nord is an example of a real thing created through engineering (ie through 50% magic, 25% imagination and 25% symbolism). The Gare du Nord is neither a bridge nor a roadway, but it was constructed by the Bridge and Roadway Engineers company between 1861 and 1864. It has a U-shaped terminus.

It features 23 female statues. That's unusual, you might think, knowing that the vast majority of statues worldwide honour men. It's not so unusual once you know that these 23 female statues do not honour specific women but instead represent cities. Hmm.

As noted in *Tante Fran's May 68 Book Club Choose Your Own Revolution*, the support pillars for the station came from a Glasgow foundry: P & W MacLellan of the Clutha Iron Works, who also made ironwork for other railway stations and bridges.

That's enough of engineering for now - time to head over to the Latin Quarter! Go to page 20.

THE LATIN QUARTER

The three new friends wound their way up the staircase, rising every higher above the street noise. 'There!' Charmian announced, flinging open a wooden door and dropping her suitcase at her feet, where it formed an immediate trip hazard for Sylva and Fran. 'Charmant,' announced Sylva. 'I must unpack immediately. Revolutionaries keep their affairs in order.' Soon the narrow wardrobe in a corner of the room held three sets of clothes: shapeless but stylish Melbourne shifts, chic printed German dresses, and revolutionary turtlenecks, slacks, black jackets and berets.

'Now,' Sylva announced, 'we drink.' Fran and Charmian grinned at each other.

'How about we start at the café at the bottom of this building?' Fran suggested. 'I saw they had a special on red wine. And if I'm not mistaken there was a bookshelf there too.'

Soon the three friends had grabbed a table on the footpath outside their building and were excitedly filling each other in on their back stories. Sylva was just pouring the last drops from the carafe of red wine when her elbow was roughly jostled. Out of nowhere, a crowd of young men with beards had appeared running pell-mell down the street and yelling.

'What the fuck?' said Charmian. Fran furrowed her eyebrows and scanned the crowd. 'There - she looks sensible. We should ask her what is going on.'

Sylva and Charmian followed the direction of Fran's brow and saw a tall, young Black woman with an Afro. Her American accent rang across the crowd as she chanted 'It is forbidden to forbid!'

'The philosophy is on point,' confirmed Sylva. The young woman seemed to sense the interest of the group at the table, and she rushed over to them.

'Do any of you have a pen? I need to refresh my slogan,' she said, pointing to her sign.

'I have pens AND paper,' said Charmian, rummaging in her capacious tote. 'And we'd love to help. But what's going on? I'm Charmian, by the way.'

'DeNanielle,' the woman introduced herself. 'What's going on is that the people have had enough. Enough of the boring, staid politicians, enough of the police who are just the tools of the boring elite. We want more out of this life. More joy. More music. More sexiness.

More freedom. More books by women. It's time for revolution!'

'This is the call of my heart, too,' said Sylva. 'Do you have time to talk a little more with us, so that maybe we can join forces?'

There was an empty fourth chair at the table, and Sylva had already magicked up a second carafe of red wine. DeNanielle grinned. 'Well, recruiting for the cause is important and thirsty work. Besides, I could really use the advice of some smart women on this ... situation I've got into with a guy. A philosopher. A philosopher Guy. I mean his name is Guy. Guy de Guy. He won't leave me alone ... '

Charmian rolled her eyes. 'Tell us everything,' she demanded. 'We are the Book Club!'

Just as DeNanielle opened her mouth to do so, the waiter ran up to their table. 'Je suis desolé, mesdemoiselles, but the cafe is closing now. It is too dangerous for us to stay open in the midst of this civil unrest.'

DeNanielle rose, tucking the carafe of wine under her arm. 'It's OK,' she told the others, 'come with me. I know a place.'

Do you want to follow DeNanielle immediately? Go to page 29.

Or do you want to find out a little bit more about one of those back stories first? Go to page 25.

CHARMIAN'S
BACKSTORY

Charmian took a swig of red wine from the thick glass tumbler on the café table. 'My back story?' she said. 'It's nothing special.'

'I was born in January 1949 in the front room of my parents' sheep station. Yes - I'm part of the squattocracy, the Australian upper class that has grown rich from the sheep's back and the violent dispossession of First Nations peoples. My father, John, had grown up observing the hideous racism that was the motor of Australian settler economic growth, but my mother Amy's private school education in Melbourne had sheltered her from such direct knowledge. She was politically ignorant the night she attended a Bachelor and Spinsters ball at the barn in Bacchus Marsh, met my father, and fell in love. But reality hit soon after their marriage, and after I was born my parents packed a carpet bag, took the train, and renounced their land claim.

They moved to a small rented shack on the Mornington Peninsula where my mother's wit and my father's cooking skills made them a magnet for local intellectuals, politicians and artists. Every night I would sit under the table, playing with paper dolls and listening to discourses on modernism or bushrangers. As I grew older, I sat at the table too, a book of ancient Greek plays or poetry in my hand, half listening and half participating. That's how I met George. We were both set to attend the University of Melbourne and study classics and journalism together. But then ... everything changed.

Harold Holt was the Prime Minister, and naturally he came to my parents' house for lunch frequently. He loved to swim, snorkel and dive at the nearby beach. That day, the 17th of December 1967 - just a few months ago - he had risen early and was on his way to our house. He stopped off at a general store to buy peanuts, insect repellent, and newspapers: one of the paper's headlines read "PM Advised to Swim Less." It was a beautiful crisp morning and he wanted to work up an appetite before lunch, so he stopped off at the beach. Passersby later said they saw a submarine briefly surface. The Bunurong people tell of the mermaids who swim there. Holt did not hesitate. He struck out for the deep water, never raising an arm to indicate distress, never showing any signs of struggle. A woman who saw him said he was "taken out like a leaf ... so quick."

After the Prime Minister's disappearance, the memorial service and the media frenzy, my parents decided I should leave the country for a time. Greece, they thought. George would go too. We could restore ourselves on a small island, perhaps meet some singer-songwriters, and hone our writing craft. That's where I'm on my way to. But first, I had to meet my pen pal, Fran. Which brings me to Paris. Here. May 68.'

So it must be time to head to a bookshop and see if they have any travel books ... go to page 29.

THE BOOKSHOP

DeNanielle lifted the carafe to her lips and took a swig, then pointed across the grey cobblestoned square. 'There it is!'

'Isn't that another café?' said Charmian. 'No,' said DeNanielle. 'Look past the burgundy awnings and cane furniture. It's on the other side.'

Charmian peered. She could just make out some plain windows, grey walls, and a small sign swinging beneath a brightly coloured little space invader. 'Editions Editions,' she read aloud, 'Is that what I think it is?'

'A bookshop!' declared Sylva. 'The true home of revolution!'

Fran frowned, but not because she didn't like bookshops. Her shoes had not coped with the cobblestones at all, and she could feel a blister developing. She bent down and rubbed her ankle. 'I hope it has a reading nook,' Fran murmured. 'Perhaps armchairs, and an in-store cafe. And soothing music.'

DeNanielle's voice cut across Fran's futuristic dreams. 'Not just a bookshop - but also a future publishing house. Come, you have to meet Kurt.'

The women tripped across the pedestrian crossing, then DeNanielle pushed the door open with confidence. 'It's Book Club time!' she announced, cutting across the strains of 'Rain and Tears' rising from the record player. It was the song of the summer, and its tinny homage to Pachelbel's Canon was already deeply ingrained in the women's minds. Years from now, whenever they heard it, it would transport them back instantly to those giddy days on the streets of Paris, its cafés, lecture halls and bookstores, bookstores like this one …

A young man looked up from reading a book behind the counter. 'DeNanielle,' he said quietly, pushing his glasses back up his nose and stroking a barely emerging beard. 'You and your friends are always welcome.'

'This is Kurt,' DeNanielle announced. 'He arrived in Paris from Algeria a couple of months ago. I've decided he's the only non-narcissist in the revolution.'

Kurt laughed quietly. 'My passion is sharing the words of others. Particularly left-wing philosophers, and even more particularly the strong voices of thinkers who have been marginalized and oppressed through systemic inequity and violence.' He gestured at the shelves around him. 'That's why I love bookselling. And perhaps, one day, I will publish some of these strong voices myself.' He looked longingly at the stack of blank paper and the stapler on his desk. The means of production. If only he had the right idea for his first book ...

'We need a place to sit and talk,' said De-Nanielle. 'Ok if we take the sofas in the storeroom? Oh, and before we sit down ... any good books we should know about?'

'Of course,' said Kurt. 'It's a good idea to do some reflecting in the midst of action. And to engage in meaningful dialogue with one another - that is also good. There are those in the revolution who talk without listening. The men of La Méthode, the men of the Odéon ... yikes.' He shuddered. But then his face brightened. 'And I have just the book for you! It's a memoir of Afrofuturism.'

He picked up a shiny paperback from a stack beside the counter. Unlike the usual French titles, it wasn't monochrome, but featured a glossy image of a young woman with sharp haircut and piercing eyes staring out at the reader.

'Janelle Monáe,' read DeNanielle softly, flicking through the first pages. 'A paean to pansexual creativity. Interesting … '

'Now where were we,' asked Sylva, flopping into the brown couch at the end of the tiny storeroom at the back of the shop. 'I believe the mermaids had just taken the Australian Prime Minister.'

'Yes, that's right,' nodded Charmian. The women talked and gossiped as the shadows through the musty shop windows lengthened, learning not only of Australian politics but also of Czechoslovak poetry and DeNanielle's love triangle with two leading Situationists. It was some time later when Charmian's voice cut through and wakened Kurt from his publishing daydreams … 'And that was as far as that went with the singer-songwriter, although we have plans to meet in Greece.'

'There's a good book about Greece,' said Kurt, 'but I don't have it in stock. I believe it's out of print. You might like to try the library?'

'Excellent idea,' said Sylva. 'Come on Charmian, let's find the library.'

'I think I might need to find some new shoes before I do any more walking,' confessed Fran.

'Shoes!' echoed DeNanielle.

Shoes (go to page 35), or the library (go to page 39)? Choose carefully.

THE SHOE SHOP

'Ding-a-ling!' A bell tinkled at the door as Fran and DeNanielle entered the shoe shop. The promise of the shop's windows, which they'd been figuratively licking before they pushed open the door, was immediately fulfilled. All around them displayed on the shelves were shoes and boots of all different colours, shapes and sizes, but with one thing in common ...

'Stylish *and* comfortable,' exclaimed Fran, lightly caressing a bright green sling back with cut-outs at the toe.

DeNanielle picked up a white patent knee-high boot. 'They sure are sister! Look at these! I know some feminists look down on fashion, but I've always thought snappy dressing and revolution go hand in hand ... '

'Mais bien sûr, mesdemoiselles,' spoke a soft voice from the back of the shop. 'But perhaps pieds à pieds, in this instance. S'il vous plait, look around, try them on, let me know your sizes. I will bring you the left shoes.'

Fran and DeNanielle turned to the voice, and saw the proprietor of the shop, a bright smile on her face and a well-worn paperback in her hand.

'Oh, you read,' asked Fran. 'What is the book? I love reading! And your shoes!'

The shoe shop owner held out the copy to Fran, its plain white front and back covers offering no clue to its contents, apart from the title, *ZAZIE DANS LE METRO*.

'You know it? Zazie is very, how do you say ... mischievous ... There's a film too, a great scene on the Tour Eiffel. You must have already ascended our Iron Lady?'

Fran and DeNanielle looked at each other, shaking their heads. 'Um, no,' replied De-Nanielle. 'Fran has only just arrived and I've been busy writing slogans.'

'I understand, mes choux,' replied the shoe shop owner. 'But don't forget to have fun in our city of love, n'est-ce pas?'

'N'EST-CE PAS!' replied Fran and De-Nanielle, their American and German accents beautifully combining.

The shoe shop owner smiled. 'Now, those left shoes, which do you want?'

***

Several hours later, Fran and DeNanielle emerged from the shop arm in arm, carrying several boxes of shoes under the other.

'What next sister?' asked DeNanielle, pulling on her new boots. 'I fancy a drink.'

'Me too, choosing from all those beauties was thirsty work. Plus I got some great careers advice!' replied Fran. 'But I wonder if we should try and catch up with others at the library first?'

You must go to the library. Don't worry, you'll get a drink later. Go to page 39.

THE LIBRARY

They burst through the doors of the library, chatting about books and the perfidiousness of men.

'Ssssshhhh!' a bespectacled man with a white moustache at the entrance desk enunciated theatrically, his finger on his lips. 'Ceci c'est la bibliothèque, mesdemoiselles. Silence!'

'Sorry!' whispered Charmian. 'But isn't this the library?'

'Mais non, c'est la bibliothèque! At the librairie books are *sold*. Here ... ' he gestured towards the serried ranks of shelving, 'you can *borrow* them ... for free!'

Charmian and Sylva nodded approvingly, and looked into the building, sensing its calm and the centuries of knowledge within.

'I am looking for a book on Greece,' asked Sylva. 'Can you help?'

'Ask over there,' he pointed into the dark of the library towards another desk. 'She will help you.'

'Merci monsieur!' chorused Sylva and Charmian. 'Just to warn you, the rest of the Book Club may be joining us soon ... '

The man lifted his eyebrows, and shrugged.

Fifty per cent of the Book Club headed over to the desk pointed out to them, occasionally distracted by a fusty smelling volume on a shelf, pulling it down to sniff the pages.

'Oh look, the bateaux-mouches!' laughed a voice ahead of them. Charmian and Sylva span round towards the information desk, to see a woman their own age, with a shock of curly red hair and snub nose. She was pointing out of the window to the Seine. 'Books and boats, two of my favourite things!'

Charmian and Sylva smiled back, detecting a fellow traveller in the mischievous face of the library assistant.

'Can I help you?'

'Yes please!' replied Sylva. 'A friend sent us ... I am looking for a book.'

'Magnifique! You've come to the right place. Just let me power up the ordinateur, and I'll find it. Do you have the book number?'

'The book number?' responded Sylva quizzically. 'Just the author and the title, I'm afraid.'

'Oh, that's a shame. We've just started using International Standard Book Numbers. What an innovation! They came from Ireland. They'll be used throughout the world soon - mark my words!'

Charmian and Sylva looked at each other in surprise. 'I suppose the world is changing in all regards,' said Charmian.

'Oh yes,' replied the librarian cheerily. 'I'm Julie, by the way. I'm also studying for a PhD in Information Sciences at the Sorbonne. I'm developing a framework for calculating the most efficient way of getting books from A to B. People talk a lot about writing and reading, but they're not the difficult part.'

Chairman and Sylva nodded, impressed. 'Tell us more!' said Sylva.

'One day, using this,' Julie gestured at the computer, 'I hope we will be able to deliver books from not just A to B, but to the Amazon! Imagine, if you can, someone in the middle of the forest, tapping on the keys and ordering a book, and POUF! It appears ...'

'Extraordinary!' said an out-of-breath voice behind them. It was DeNanielle and Fran, bundling bags of shoes behind them.

'Have you got the book, Sylva?' asked Fran.

'Here it is,' said Julie, handing a slim volume to the Book Club. 'Check out is at the front desk. Where are you going now, readers? It's not time yet, but you should join us at the Sorbonne later. Or if you're busy, we'll be meeting up afterwards in Montmartre. There'll be a show you don't want to miss ...'

The Book Club looked at each other, considering their options.

'I definitely need a drink,' said DeNanielle. 'What was the name of that cafe Kurt mentioned ... ?

'La Méthode, I think?' replied Fran.

Julie shrugged. 'If you must ... but there's also this sixteenth-century cellar I know ... '

Do you want to drink at La Méthode? Go to page 68.

Or the Cave des Vins? Go to page 45.

CAVE DES VINS

The women hurtled down the tiny spiral staircase at the back of the wine shop, coming to an abrupt halt at the base. The dim, cool cellar was divided into dim alcoves and spanned by stone archways.

'Oh cool - is that what I think it is?' said DeNanielle, running into a shadowy corner. A white plastic machine whirred and hummed.

'Depends what you think it is, and what it is,' said Fran sensibly.

DeNanielle was lifting the lid. 'It looks like a roneo mimeograph,' she said, 'but it's more advanced than any I've ever seen. The ink is BRIGHT purple.'

'So we can make more copies,' declared a voice. Kurt stepped forward from another nearby shadowy corner, stroking his beard (which was getting longer by the day). 'There are more of these up in the Institute of Beaux Arts, but I keep a few advanced machines down here to spread the risk. The revolution needs its printed ephemera!'

'Its flowering of flyers!' Sylva chimed in.

'This screen printing draws on the flat iconography of stencils to truly democratise art, just as we want to democratise society. Anonymous art! Down with aestheticism! No value judgements!' declaimed DeNanielle.

Kurt nodded. 'I love to print these...but even more, I love to effectively distribute them. My academic mentors, including Pyer Burdye, have never paid sufficient attention to the im-

portance of distribution in cultural production.'

Charmian took a note of this using the pencil she always carried. It seemed to her that
distribution would be even more of a challenge
in Australia than for Paris, a metropolis at the
centre of Europe.

Kurt continued, 'We shall take distribution
to the streets. But also - beneath the streets.
That's right,' he said, twisting open a circular
concrete porthole and pointing beyond it, 'to
the sewers!'

Sylva screwed her nose up a little. 'Um,
maybe I could take some with me to the Tour
Eiffel instead?'

Fran looked torn. 'Both,' she said, 'are engineering marvels that could play a role in distribution. What to do?'

Do you want to take the Métro to the Tour Eiffel? Go to page 53.

Or to enter the sewers? Go to page 49.

THE SEWERS

Three quarters of the Book Club and Kurt edged along the narrow wall, barely daring to look into the frothy brown water as it raced through the channel just below them. The low lighting also revealed graffiti on the walls: enormous rats heralding revolution; more slogans; and a number of arrows heading in contradictory directions.

'It really pongs down here,' said Charmian, wrinkling her nose in disgust.

Fran rooted in her tote and pulled out a silk scarf, which she tied over her mouth and nose. DeNanielle put down her shoe boxes precariously on the edge of the brown water, and un-laced the length of material she had through her belt loops. 'Also useful in riots,' she smiled, as she pulled the mask over her lower face. Kurt drew a spotty handkerchief from his jacket breast pocket.

Fran and Charmian turned to each other and shrugged.

'Which way?' said DeNanielle, picking up her boxes from the ground.

'Hmm, I think this way,' indicated Kurt down a tunnel. 'But I wonder if there is a boat ... Sometimes the égoutiers give tourists a ride, for quelques sous.'

'This is certainly alternative Paris tourism,' responded Charmian. 'My postcards will be ... unusual.'

'Salut,' called DeNanielle up the tunnel, as she spotted an égoutier. 'Can you give us a lift?'

A small rowboat moved towards them, a blinding light at its front. 'Monsieur, mesdemoiselles? Voulez-vous un tour?'

'Oui - we are four, can you fit us all in? Plus some shoe boxes and leaflets ...' replied Fran.

The égoutier switched off the boat's light, revealing his muscular rower's arms and moustache. With a slow stare he looked at the party and their goods. 'For you ladies, mais oui!'

Three quarters of the Book Club rolled their six eyes simultaneously from left to right.

'D'accord, d'accord. But who is he?' asked the égoutier.

'Oh, he's just Kurt!' the women chorused.

'But my leaflets ... ! I need to take them to Guy de Guy at the dojo,' replied Kurt, hurt.

'OK! But what is this leaflet?' responded the egoutier.

Kurt handed him one down to the boat, which the égoutier scrutinised carefully. 'Huh. Ouais. OUVRIERS ÉTUDIANTS UNIS NOUS VAINCRONS! I am a worker! You are students! For you, it's free!'

Kurt beamed with pleasure, as he and the three women bundled themselves into the rowboat, with soliticous help from the égoutier, who stowed the leaflets and shoes carefully beneath his seat. 'How you say ... precious cargo!'

The égoutier gently dipped his oars into the effluviant. 'But where to, les camarades? There is an exit right by La Tour Eiffel I can take you to (go to page 53), or should I take you to Guy de Guy? (go to page 68).'

LA TOUR EIFFEL

Well-shod feet on the ground, noses turned up in the air, the women stood open-mouthed underneath the Eiffel Tower.

'It's … big!' said Fran, closing the cover of the manhole they'd just emerged from.

'And strong!' added Charmian.

'And beautiful!' completed DeNanielle. 'And a lady… But where's Sylva? I've got the tickets already.'

The Book Club spotted their fourth member running towards them, waving a sheaf of papers.

'There she is! Come on Sylva! Sewers beat the Métro!'

Sylva laughed. 'OK, you win! With the smell of effluent in your noses ... Time for tourism?'

The other women assented, and turned their attention to the engineering feat above them.

***

One thousand, six hundred and sixty-five steps later, the Book Club stood on the very top parapet of Gustave Eiffel's pig iron miracle.

'Oof,' breathed Sylva. 'That was quite the climb ...'

Fran beamed at her friend. 'But look at the view ...'

All of Paris was arrayed below them; broad boulevards, parks, hills, glistening churches, and the Seine cutting through the middle.

'Smoke!' cried Charmian, pointing to the south. 'The protests are starting again ...'

'REVOLUTION!' cried DeNanielle, grabbing the leaflets Charmian had carried up the stairs, and flinging them into the wind.

The women cheered.

'What next?' asked Fran.

'I think I fancy more sightseeing. I've hardly done any since I arrived. How about one of those boats?' DeNanielle gestured towards the river.

'Hmm, I've got a contact at Nanterre to go and interview,' responded Charmian. 'Do you want to come, Sylva?'

Do you join Fran and DeNanielle on a bateau-mouche? Go to page 63.

or head to Nanterre with Charmian and Sylva? Go to page 60.

Or for those of you interested in engineering, find out more about La Tour Eiffel? Go to page 57.

ENGINEERING MANUAL: LA TOUR EIFFEL

Dear reader, do you know what one of the engineering marvels of the engineering world is? The Tour Eiffel.

The Tour is 1,050 feet high. The 'foot' unit of measurement is supposedly based on the size of Charlemagne's foot. Charlemagne was crowned Holy Roman Emperor in 800 and died in 814.

Modern France tends not to use feet but instead to use the metric system. In which case, the Tour Eiffel is 330 metres high. That's taller than it used to be, because its height was augmented by the addition of antennae in 1957. Antennae were also added in 2000 and 2022, but that's in the future.

The Tour Eiffel is made of wrought iron, 7,000 tonnes of it (remarkably it is lighter than the air that surrounds it!), connected with 2.5 million rivets. From 1887, horse-drawn carts carried pre-assembled sections to the site where workers assembled the Tour Eiffel.

The site engineering.com notes that 'nothing remotely like it has ever been constructed' and that engineer Gustave Eiffel earned the nickname 'magician of iron.'

In addition to inspiring awe and wonder and providing great views across Paris, the tower has practical uses like measuring the speed of wind and transmitting radio.

Magnifique!

Well, now you know all that, do you want to join Fran and DeNanielle on a bateau-mouche (go to page 63). Or head to Nanterre with Charmian and Sylva (go to page 60)?

NANTERRE

Half an hour later, Charmian and Sylva stepped onto the streets of Nanterre, far from the tourist sights of central Paris. Charmian took out her spiral bound notebook and pencil, and started scribbling.

Students heading purposefully onto campus
Polo necks ...
Serious faces ...
Smoking ...
Umbrellas ...
A book under every arm ...

'Umbrellas?' broke in Sylva, staring at the sunny skies.

'Weird,' said Charmian. 'Let's follow them, and find my contact. He's called Daniel Cohn-Bendit.'

They joined the stream of students into a lecture theatre, and took seats at the back. On the blackboard at the front, written up in perfect chalk cursive, the words 'Intro à la Sociologie'.

The students placed their books on their desks. '*Les heritiers*', read Charmian. 'Students and culture ...'

A middle-aged professor walked to the front of the class, placing a sheaf of papers on the lectern. The students hushed, but then a figure with a shock of curly red hair stood up at the front of the lecture hall, and started shouting, 'WE WANT A NEW AND ORIGINAL WORLD! WE WILL NOT PERISH OF BOREDOM!! UNTER DEN TALAREN DER MUFF VON TAUSEND JAHREN!!!'

All around him, students raised umbrellas above their heads, opening and shutting them, chanting slogans excitedly.

'Who's that?' asked Sylva to the young woman sitting next to her, while Charmian furiously scribbled down notes.

The woman turned to her and smiled, 'Dany the Red, of course ... Come on, we're going into the streets now - we're heading to join our comrades in the Latin Quarter ...'

Sylva elbowed Charmian in the ribs. 'Charmian, that's him! Let's go!'

The students noisily filed out of the hall, leaving the professor at the front of the class, bemused. Charmian and Sylva followed. Go to page 68.

BOAT(S) ON THE SEINE

'I have always had a weakness for boats,' declared Fran, running breathlessly down the staircase towards the Seine. 'Ferries, of course. Sewer boats. Paddle steamers. And now - river boats!'

DeNanielle nodded in agreement, puffing a little. The two of them had run from the Tour Eiffel to the river. These shoes were built for speed! (while still being stylish). 'I love boats too. And the bateaux-mouches are iconic,' she told Fran, once she'd caught her breath. 'They always have been, from the moment of their origin in the nineteenth century in the Mouche district of Lyon.'

'Someone will no doubt add that information to my Wee Kit-Pedia.' Fran patted the pocket where she kept the little book of facts. If only the book were ... a narrower rectangle. With maybe a cover made of glass. And you could turn the pages by touching the cover with your finger and swiping. Could it play music as well? Talking voices?

'A pod ... that casts ...' she murmured.

'What's that?' DeNanielle asked. She was distracted turning her pockets inside out looking for coins.

'And you could pay for tickets with it too ...' Fran was lost in her utopian slash dystopian dream until DeNanielle laughed and clicked her fingers. 'Snap snap! Time to catch a boat!'

Before they knew it they were up on the top deck of the squat rectangular boat, eyes drifting upwards to the cloudless May sky and cheeks brushed by the warm breezes of Paris in the springtime. A small band of troubadours set themselves up at the front of the boat, crooning Serge Gainsbourg songs to the accompaniment of an accordion and a violin. A roving salesman sold DeNanielle and Fran glasses of red wine and cheese platters, turning the boat trip into the most perfect sort of picnic. Paris unrolled on either side of them: the Left Bank to one side, the Right Bank to the other. And in between? Water and boats.

'Ah, the boating life,' sighed Fran with happiness.

'Is that the Louvre? Is that the Odéon? Is that a book stall?' DeNanielle's questions bubbled up amidst her excitement with the sights she was seeing. The two could have chattered and dreamed and imagined their way through Paris' boating life forever, but it was not to be. Squinting into the sun, DeNanielle saw it first, looking darkly to starboard. 'Is that ... a man-boat?'

'Ugh,' grunted Fran. 'A boat full of men. Let me guess, they are explaining things.'

'There does seem to be a lot of talking going on. But wait. What's that to port?'

'A ... ladyboat?' This cheerful apparition lifted Fran's spirits considerably. 'What are they waving?'

'It seems to be signs and posters, inviting everyone to the Sorbonne for philosophical, social and political discussions! And they say there'll be cheese there!'

'Right let's go! I think the bateau-mouche stops right near the Sorbonne, we can hop off there.'

'Or,' Fran said wryly, 'we could follow the men.'

The bateau-mouche captain interjected 'I think that man has stolen a tablecloth from La Méthode. There's a bateau-mouche stop near there too ...'

I guess you'd better deal with that stolen tablecloth. Go to page 68.

LA MÉTHODE

The Book Club burst noisily through the doors of the cafe Kurt had told them about, chattering about their latest reads.

'My method is drinking!' screeched Sylva, commandeering a tableclothed table by the bar. The others grabbed chairs and dropped their bags to the tiled floor, scanning around them at the burnished wooden bar and ceiling beams.

Several owl-like faces atop of black turtle-necks turned towards them from the next table. Cigarettes lazily dropping from left hands, a glass of red in each right. A pile of leaflets were scattered across the table. 'Welcome, camarades!', announced one of the men, his white woollen jumper distinguishing him from the others as the leader of the pack. 'This is La Méthode ... You are new in town?'

DeNanielle shook her head, while the other three nodded enthusiastically at the bespectacled, bowl-cut figure in front of them.

'Join us,' invited the leader, as the rest of the men leaned in around him. 'I am Guy de Guy.' DeNanielle rolled her eyes. The other men nodded, shuffling their chairs even closer to each other to make way for the women.

The women looked at each other and shrugged, pulling their chairs up to the men's table.

'I was just explaining how in societies where modern conditions of production prevail, all of life presents itself as an immense accumulation of spectacles,' pronounced Guy de Guy.

The other men nodded sagely. 'And that every-thing that was directly lived has moved away into a representation.'

The Book Club looked at each other, per-plexed. 'Do you mean that ...' began DeNanielle.

'That's right,' interrupted Guy de Guy. 'The spectacle is the nightmare of imprisoned mod-ern society which ultimately expresses noth-ing more than its desire to sleep. The spectacle is the guardian of sleep.'

Charmian yawned, remembering it was only several hours ago that she had stepped off the plane from Melbourne.

'So ...' said Fran.

'Correct,' replied Guy de Guy, calling the waiter over to the table, and finishing his wine. 'Do you know I think I have drunk much more than most people who drink. And written less than most people who write.' He laughed at his own joke, as the waiter approached, leaning his sweeping brush against the wall.

'Garçon,' Guy de Guy said. 'Drinks for the ladies please! Red wine? A little pastis?'

The waiter coughed. 'It's Kurt, remember.' He smiled at the Book Club in recognition. 'Welcome to La Méthode, Guten Tag, Fran. I'm glad you've come, you'll cheer up my shift. Have you had a good day?'

The women nodded vigorously. 'Mais oui!' cried Charmian, her tiredness forgotten. 'It's so exciting, with everything going on in the streets ...'

'Oh yes,' broke in Guy de Guy. 'HUMANITY WON'T BE HAPPY TILL THE LAST BUREAU-CRAT IS HUNG WITH THE GUTS OF THE LAST CAPITALIST'.

All the other men (apart from Kurt) started shouting slogans.

'OCCUPY THE FACTORIES!'

'POWER TO THE WORKERS COUNCILS!'

'NEVER WORK!'

'ABOLISH ALIENATION!'

'DEATH TO THE COPS!'

'RED-HEADS FOREVER!'

'No more gig economy,' whispered Kurt.

'Yee ha!' chimed in DeNanielle. 'I agree. But what about those drinks ...'

Kurt smiled. 'Normally I recommend a Campari and soda. But can I bring you something I've just invented? It's based on an old recipe I found in Firenze ...'

The women nodded enthusiastically, and shortly they held in their hands a bright red drink. Each took a slurp and their eyes widened. 'CRIKEY', said Charmian, raising her glass to the table.

'To the revolution!'

Everyone held aloft their glasses, chinking them merrily as they toasted the revolution.

'Now, where was I?' asked Guy de Guy. 'Ah yes, all that was directly lived has become more representation. And quotations are useful in periods of ignorance or obscurantist beliefs ...'

The men leaned in once more, while the women looked at each other as he continued to explain something about tourism and the leisure of going to see the banal canal.

Fran whispered to her friends, 'Shall we stay? These drinks are marvellous, but I'm not sure how much more men explaining things I can take.'

DeNanielle nodded, 'I agree, sister, he is irritating. But his work is important. He also wrote somewhere that in order to write we must read, and to read we must live. That's a maxim I can get on board with. Although oddly he doesn't like reading. Just living, writing ... and drinking.'

You now have several choices ...

Do you want to go on a dérive to a different bar? Go to page 45.

Do you want to carry on listening to men explaining things? Go to page 75.

Or do you want to hear some women explaining things? Go to page 78.

L'ODÉON

The tall columns of the Odéon Theatre reared up behind the group of scruffy, bespectacled and bearded young men gathered on its steps. A hand painted banner across the façade proclaimed in red letters, L'ODÉON EST OUVERT. And ouvert it was. Leaflets scattered in the gutters nearby proclaimed the event: 'After the police occupation of the Latin Quarter and Nanterre! After the barricades and the savage police repression! We occupy the Odéon, symbol of a bourgeois culture we fundamentally contest!'

The Book Club members settled on a step to listen, turning their collars up against the chill of the wind that roared through the gaps between columns and trying not to get trampled by the people streaming through the arched doorways. On a step nearby, a man with fierce red eyebrows and a turtleneck periodically shouted into a megaphone, 'Behold as the professionals of the spectacle at the Odéon join us, students and workers, in our strike!'

Glimpses of the inside of the theatre showed speeches happening amongst the red velvet chairs. And outside the theatre, speeches ran on a loop as men continually explained society and the revolution to passersby and themselves. One brushed his dark hair away from his eyes and started pointing vigorously. 'The ideas of the ruling class are in every epoch the ruling idea. This whole semblance must come to its natural end and society cease at last to be organised in the form of class-rule.' He paused for a sip of red wine, and wiped the side of his mouth.

Dawn brightened to midday, which length-ened into evening and night.

'Three principal characteristics of bureau-cracy,' continued the same man, or perhaps a different one, 'are that it controls political power, it controls the means of production and it rules in the name of the proletariat. The rise of a pacifying bureaucracy is a fatality.'

The Book Club nodded every now and then. They didn't disagree. But they also wondered if they were trapped in some kind of existential vortex, doomed to hear men explain things forever (go to page 68).

Was there any escape? Maybe, even, women explaining things? (go to page 78).

SORBONNE

The four women rounded the cobblestoned corner and were confronted by the vast grey bulk of the Sorbonne. Tall windows peered down on the street, and narrow portals led to what they presumed was an internal courtyard.

'The seat of knowledge is quite forbidding, no?' said Sylva, smoothing her hair thoughtfully.

DeNanielle nodded. 'Normally, there's guards at the gate, too. But can you hear that?'

The four women turned their heads, robot quartet like, to the left. A small crowd had gathered around a woman who was scrawling on the Sorbonne wall with chalk.

TO SEE LIFE WITH NEW EYES

The woman whirled around, shaking her pixie haircut and glaring fiercely at the crowd. 'The primary terrains of creativity in the future will be experiments in behavior and the construction of complete settings, moments of life freely created - new situations!' she declared. She winked at DeNanielle.

'Oh. My. God,' said Sylva. 'Do you know who that is? Michèle Bernstein! The O.G. situationist, author of much of the journal of the Situationiste Internationale! She's brilliant.'

'Yes, what she is saying is really smart,' said Fran. 'In fact, it gives me a few ideas for things to do back home in Frankfurt.'

'Look,' cried Charmian. 'It's happening all up and down the street!' Sure enough, now that the women looked there were small groups everywhere, impromptu classrooms assembled on the streets outside the Sorbonne, as women scribbled on walls and delivered impassioned speeches about the need for intellectual and cultural change.

'If this is happening outside, what's happening INSIDE?' Charmian continued. 'I'm going to find out!'

'Wait just a minute,' DeNanielle said. 'Two seconds. I must share the words of my hero Angela Davis with these women.' She whipped a piece of chalk out of her back pocket and yelled to the street. 'JUSTICE IS INDIVISIBLE!' The words flew out of her hand and mouth at the same time. 'As Angela Davis says, we are at an important moment for activism, for giving back and not considering ourselves as single individuals but as part of an ongoing historical movement! In America, where I am from, there is a battle for the recognition of civil rights. These must apply to all! We cannot decide who gets them and who doesn't.' The Book Club nodded and cheered, along with twenty or so others who had clustered around DeNanielle. 'You have to act as if it were possible to radically transform the world. And you have to do it all the time.' More nods. 'What's more, the revolution must go deep!' De-Nanielle declaimed. 'We have to liberate minds as well as society.'

Another Black woman stepped up next to DeNanielle. 'Revolution must be intersectional or it is nothing,' she said firmly. 'Revolution for the White men in berets at La Méthode is not enough.'

'Right on! And I'll be right back,' DeNanielle said to the crowd. 'I've just got to check out the inside of the Sorbonne with my Book Club.'

The four women passed through the portal and into a large shadowy hall. A woman in her

60s was on the podium, softly lit and surrounded by dancing dust motes as she gave an oration. 'Simone de Beauvoir,' breathed Charmian. 'The woman, the legend.' The hall was filled with murmuring assent and conversation as the crowd of women engaged in the deep philosophical work of reconceptualising the world around them.

'Each of us is responsible for everything and to every human being. I am incapable of conceiving infinity, and yet I do not accept finity. I want this adventure that is the context of my life to go on without end. Empty and unlimited, we seek from within our nothingness to attain All.'

Charmian and Fran took some cheese and saucisson from the generously laden table at the back of the hall. 'So this is the real revolution,' said Sylva. 'The dismantling of gender hierarchies, of race-based discrimination, the chance to breathe and see anew. Finally!'

'Hey, it's Kurt!' exclaimed DeNanielle. The four women raced to the back of the room, where Kurt was busily taking notes.

'Hi gang,' he beamed. 'I've got it! The idea for a book that is so important it demands the establishment of a publishing house. It will be an anthology of feminist revolutionary essays from Paris May 68, capturing these important ideas and sharing them with the world.'

'Genius,' affirmed Charmian. 'We will discuss it at our Book Club in due course.'

A young woman with curly hair sitting nearby piped up. 'If you want to get a copy to Australia, you'll need a good distribution system. Maybe I can help, I'm a librarian.'

'Julie!' cried Charmian. 'Merci!'

Kurt's face lit up. 'This is exactly the knowledge I need! May I speak to you further about this ...?'

'Sorry to interrupt, but is that a Sorbonne guard?' blurted out DeNanielle, 'And are they joining the audience, or coming to quash us?'

'I guess time will tell,' shrugged Fran. 'But perhaps it's time for us to do something. Words demand action, after all! And sometimes also more words.'

***

These speeches aren't very gender diverse. Is this reverse sexism? What do the men think? Go to page 68.

Otherwise, time to riot!!!!!! Go to page 85.

BIG RIOT

They turned the corner from the Sorbonne. The wide, grey cobblestoned avenue seemed to stretch for miles in the cool light of evening. All the little shops lining the street had closed and locked their doors, but eyes peeped out behind from lace curtains. Down the centre of the avenue, the students and workers marched.

UNDER THE STREET, THE BEACH!
THIS CONCERNS ALL OF US!

The Book Club ran into the crowd, joining in the shouting and linking arms with other comrades. This was revolution! And about time too! Society needed a shake-up.

Charmian and Sylva had been handed banners to wave, and twirled the long poles energetically. DeNanielle yelled out to the man beside her, 'Put me on your shoulders!' Up she went, and threw her hands in the air. Every now and then, the Book Club members caught each other's eyes and grinned. They might not have a full and complete grasp of French philosophising (yet), but they knew enough to know what mattered. Progress. Equality. The genuine exchange of ideas. Fran looked up at the buildings of the Sorbonne and mused on the change that was coming. Knowledge for all.

Suddenly, a wave of nerves rippled through the protest. The police had come from nowhere, advancing down the wide and unfriendly avenue towards the young people. Heavy black helmets and thick goggles were visible above the interlinked shields, interspersed with batons. The machinery of the state was brutal. The protestors had to act fast.

BUILD SOME BARRICADES!

The first tear gas bombs ripped into the crowd of students. Wails of pain and outrage filled the air. DeNanielle pulled her scarf up over her face, and started grabbing cobblestones and piling them up to use as weapons. Fran, Sylva and Charmian ran up to a Deux Chevaux, and tipped it onto its side to hide behind. Fran cast a brief, longing look at a manhole cover - under that, she knew, lay the sewers, and a possible escape route. But she would stay with her comrades.

A haze settled over the street. Bloodcurdling shrieks and yells overlapped and became indistinguishable. Cars up and down the avenue were on fire, flames blazing and smoke curling thickly. The young people were holding their own against police brutality, sheltering behind their hastily built barricades of cobblestones, street signs, park benches and torn off doors. This revolution wasn't going to be stopped, not yet, not like this.

The Book Club lobbed their cobblestones, and ducked and weaved around their upturned car. In the distance, they could see Kurt ducking around a corner, past a wooden fence and in front of an iron grilled store to try and save a younger man from a police blow. This wasn't just a news story, Charmian thought. Real people were getting hurt. She felt an upsurge of compassion.

The long night of the barricades seemed like it would never end, but gradually the energy shifted. Groups of students, their hands clasped over the heads, were marched by police to the jails, arrested. Two ambulance officers, white bibs with red crosses flapping in the night breeze, carried an injured student on a stretcher. In moments, the streets emptied. The police retreated - vanished. Fran, Sylva, DeNanielle and Charmian were still cowering behind their little car. They gazed at each other in shock. The morning mist cleared around them, showing upturned chairs abandoned in the middle of the street. One banner still flew limply from where it had been shoved into a fire hydrant.

'We need to tend our wounds,' announced Fran. 'Let's get out of here and go somewhere safer.'

'Where we can regroup and get ready for the next action,' nodded Sylva.

'But where should we go?' asked Charmian.

'I know,' said DeNanielle. 'We need ...

Some champagne and some fun. Go to page 97.

To contemplate death. Go to page 90.

PÈRE LACHAISE

'Ah, I love death tourism!' said Sylva, as they took the route up through the archway into Père Lachaise cemetery. Grave stones and family memorials assembled on the pathway on either side as they climbed upwards. 'It's the logical end of distribution, after all.'

The others laughed. 'Death and distribution!' cried out Charmian.

'Sssshhhh, mesdemoiselles,' shouted a man in a serge uniform from the cabin at the entranceway to the cemetery. 'People are ... sleeping here.'

Fran giggled. 'Sleeping ... !'

The women climbed higher to a grand chapel, columns at its front. 'Look at the view! Le tout Paris!' cried Sylva.

The four contemplated the view, and the restful scene around them: graves, more graves, and people reading, reading, reading ...

'I heard about this one tomb,' whispered De-Nanielle after a moment of contemplation. 'Some of the women told me about it. It's ... well endowed ...'

The others looked at her in surprise. 'Lead on,' said Charmian.

A few minutes later, after some searching through the overgrown pathways, tombs of every shape and size, celebrating famous Parisian families, writers, musicians and politicians, they arrived at a statue of a recumbent man, flowers strewn across it.

'Victor Noir,' read Fran. 'Let me check his story, one moment ...' She reached into her bag and got out her Wee Kit-Pedia. 'Hmm, interesting, he was a journalist, and died in a duel. After that there were violent protests all over France!'

'Just like now!' said Sylva.

The women stared down at the statue. The bronze statue had been burnished at his lips, and then again at...

'His dick!' laughed Charmian. 'People must have been rubbing it!'

Fran carried on reading. 'The tomb is a fertility symbol, and if you rub it sexual happiness will be all yours!'

All the women laughed, uproariously, and reached out their hands.

'To sex,' they all cried.

Editor: for the sake of time (not modesty; fan fiction is strongly encouraged at this point) we draw a veil over exactly what happened next. However, it would be remiss not to mention that after this fulfilling visitation, the four women then fell upon Parmentier's tomb. Parmentier is most celebrated for popularising the potato for human consumption across Europe, and for this, we all thank him thoroughly, and leave potatoes at his tomb for a small recognition of all that he bestowed on us all, down the ages. 'To potatoes!'

This tomb was an equally satisfying experience to that offered by Victor Noir. Indeed, it is hard to say which of sex or potatoes is the better. 'To proTUBERances!'

Would you like the recipe of Hachis Parmentier? Go to page 94.

Or go to Montmartre? Go to page 97.

HACHIS PARMENTIER

All praise the potato! Merci beaucoup à Parmentier!

To make hachis Parmentier, have assembled the following:

Minced beef*
Onions
Carrots
Garlic
Herbs
Red wine
Stock
Cream
Butter

Salt and Pepper
Comté cheese
Oil

Heat the oven to a low temperature. Brown the minced beef in the oil in a large casserole dish. Remove the beef, add oil if necessary, and fry the onions, carrots and crushed garlic. Add herbs and red wine (taking a glass for yourself and your stripe-shirted sous-chef, if you have one). Add in the beef and stock, bring to the boil, put on the lid, and place in the oven for a good long time.

Boil and mash potatoes until very smooth. Add cream, butter and salt and pepper to taste. Add grated Comté (reserving a little). Take the beef out of the oven, add the mashed potato mixture to the top, smoothing it out. Add on a little more butter and grated Comté, and return to the oven for another half hour or so.

Mmmmm ... bon appetit!

*Puy lentils are a delicious and nutritious substitute for beef. However, POTATOES WILL NOT BE SUBSTITUTED.

Where now?

Drinks and a show? Let's go to the cabaret! Go to page 97.

Are we already in heaven? Go to page 110.

MONTMARTRE

T he Book Club looked up in wonder at the brightly lit, spinning blades that cut through the Paris spring night.

'Le Moulin Noir,' breathed Charmian. Neon tubes fizzed around the plywood windmill constructed atop the Montmartre club on the other side of the boulevard. The sound of saxophones wafted towards them and the velvet ropes at the open doorway beckoned invitingly.

'It is TIME for FUN!' squealed DeNanielle, and the four darted between cars and made their way to the doorway of the legendary cabaret bar.

'Wait a second,' said Charmian, 'a photobooth! Quick let's take some!' She fed some coins into the slot then grabbed her friends and jumped inside.

Laughing, they hammed it up for the camera then tumbled back outside to wait for the strip of black and white photos to emerge. 'This will be my new favourite bookmark,' Charmian declared, waving it in the air to dry.

Fran smiled, 'I'm sure I can think of a way to replicate it and distribute it amongst the club members ... now that we have learned more about production and distribution.'

Laughing, the Book Club members made their way inside the club. Julie was sitting with a group of friends at a small round table near the stage. 'Over here!' she waved at them excitedly. 'You made it!' Fran, Sylva and DeNanielle dashed over to join the curly red-haired librar-ian and what they could only assume were other book-loving women.

Charmian yelled that she'd join them in a minute. 'But first I'll get us a round of Negro-nis,' announced Charmian. 'The revolution re-quires it.'

She was elbowing her way back through the crowd when a hush fell over the room. The red velvet curtains hung across the stage twitched. The show was about to begin!

The curtains drew back, revealing on the stage a slightly built woman, dressed in a top hat and tails, plus fishnet stockings, high heels and a cane. She waved to the assembled crowd, cheerily.

'Céline!' called out Julie, 'On est là!'

Céline bowed perfomatively low to the corner of the room where the Book Club were gathered, now clutching their Negronis.

'Bonsoir, tout le monde, and welcome to Le Moulin Noir!'

A cheer came up from the assembled crowd.

'Ce soir, I will celebrate the révolution with you. We have paint! We will paint magic slogans in the air with cierges magiques!'

As Céline spoke, several waitresses arrived with trays packed with cigarettes, matches, and sparklers. 'Help yourselves, mes cheries!' called Céline, as the music became more frantic.

The book club eagerly grabbed hold of the wares, and lit the end of the sparklers.

All at once the room was lit up with the words of feminist revolution, in blue and white and red, in green and pink and orange. The Book Club twirled the sparklers over the heads, as the gentle smell of the matches filled the room.

'Vive la révolution!' shouted Celine.

'Vive la révolution!' shouted back the women.

Fran smiled to the other members of the book group. 'This is our last night. But I have an idea - we all enjoy books - it's what brought us together. But in the past few days slogans have also become part of who we are. We must add slogan-painting to the activities of our Book Club!'

Sylva, DeNanielle and Charmian lifted their Negronis to Fran's, as the sparklers continued to cast their light across Le Moulin Noir. 'To the Book and Slogan Club!'

***

Before the Book Club members are dispersed once more to the four corners of the world, there are postcards to post! Accompany them to the post office? Go to page 103.

Time to rejoin reality. Go with Fran back on the train to Frankfurt? Go to page 107.

Hold on, maybe a different future is possible? Go to page 110.

THE POST OFFICE

The sandstone arches of the P.T.T. building in Montmartre glowed softly in the streetlights. DeNanielle pointed at the blue lettered logo above the doorway: 'Postes, télégraphes et téléphones! We love media and communications. This is our kind of place.' They pushed open the door and Fran called out in happy surprise. 'Kurt!'

Kurt looked up from the worn wooden bench where he was deep in conversation with a young woman. 'My favourite Book Club, and its Zaftig leader!' he smiled. 'This is Véronique. She is just explaining distribution to me.'

Véronique laughed and shook her head under its jaunty cap. Her hands were shoved deep inside the capacious pockets of her sky blue dress, which also featured a sharp collar and a stitched logo of a paper plane (or was it a bird?). 'Distribution never sleeps! The introduction of postcodes here in France four years ago has shown just how powerful an organised system for disseminating print material can be. And now, we want to move books more effectively around the world too! Starting with this anthology of feminist philosophy that Kurt is editing.'

'Yes,' said Sylva, 'words can convey so much, if they can reach new readers - like the poetry of my country, Czechoslovakia. You should look into that for your next book, Kurt.'

'I wouldn't mind some new reading material,' agreed Fran. 'And I certainly approve of organisation.' She gazed admiringly at the tall metal pigeonhole shelving that lined the back wall of the post office.

'In the meantime, though,' interjected Charmian, 'we need to stay in touch with friends and family and share the news of all that has happened here in Paris over the past few days. I might drop a line to the newspaper editor in Melbourne, too. Got any postcards?'

Véronique laughed again. 'But of course!' She pointed to a rotating metal stand, filled to overflowing with black-and-white photographic cards featuring the Tour Eiffel, flower stands, the clubs of Montmartre, and even a boat being rowed through the sewers.

Fran ran her finger softly over their serrated cardboard edges. 'These are perfect.' Her eye was caught by one postcard featuring a photo of tubers, with a recipe printed on the back.

The Book Club members grabbed handfuls of the postcards and scrawled their messages, licking the stamps that Véronique gave them and watching in glee as she franked each one.

'Staying in touch ... sharing the written word ... let's pledge to always do it!' said Fran solemnly. The others hugged and agreed.

Somewhere outside, a clock chimed. Their next adventures beckoned.

***

Are you ready to take the train home? Go to page 107.

Or is it time for Actual Revolution? Go to page 110.

But what was the recipe on that tubers post-card? Go to page 94.

TRAIN TO FRANKFURT

Back at the Gare du Nord, the four women hugged each other amidst the crowds on the platform. They were tired but happy from their night carousing with the students and artists of Montmartre; the Negronis drunk and then the case of wine from the vineyard opened ... Who on earth knew there was a vineyard right in the middle of the city?!

'Well, I guess this is it, for now ...' said Fran, sorrowfully.

Sylva threw her arms around her friend. 'We're comrades for life now Fran. Let's meet again, next year, next decade, in some utopian future ...'

'Here's to that,' cheered DeNanielle. 'There's so much work to be done.'

'Yeah,' chipped in Charmian. 'And books to read ...'

Fran wiped a tear from her eye. 'Yes, books to read. In fact, we'll soon have Kurt's publication from the Sorbonne - how exciting!'

The women smiled at each other, as Fran's train whistled and the guard motioned at her to get on. She scrambled up the stairs, remembering her journey to Paris, just a few days ago. But so much had happened!

Fran took one last look at her three friends, waving at her on the platform. She pulled the window down and stuck her head out. 'Au revoir! A la prochaine!'

'To books! And revolution!' the three carolled back, as the train pulled away from the platform, and out of the city of lights, and love, and reading, and revolution...

THE END - OR IS IT?

Do you want to find out more about the Gare du Nord (It's not too late)? Go to page 17.

Is it finally time for ACTUAL REVOLUTION? Go to page 110.

Or do you want to hop forwards several decades to Frankfurt? Read the epilogue. Go to page 113. Although it's very similar to the prologue, if you've already read that. (Some things are circular.)

ACTUAL REVOLUTION

Fran looked out the train window, thinking of potatoes and Victor Noir. 'So, this is revolution,' she smiled to herself. The train hovered above the tracks, gliding soundlessly through the countryside. In the distance, flying cars swooshed gracefully around a village roundabout — the revolution may have transformed science, technology, engineering and the arts, but France still had more roundabouts per capita than any other European nation.

Leaning back in her seat, Fran collected her thoughts. It had all happened so quickly. The Sorbonne guards were the first sign. Why had a university ever had armed guards, anyway?

Once they laid down their weapons and joined the students and workers, others followed: the police, the army, then the politicians. All came and joined the feminist philosophers in their enlivening conversations.

That night at Le Moulin Noir, the book club had tumbled outside to discover celebrations in the street. Genuinely inclusive conversations were spreading far and wide. Obstacles were evaporating. Opportunities were opening. Within weeks, the diversity of voices debating key issues had solved most of the world's problems. Transportation systems, agriculture, and economic models were completely re-imagined. Established patterns of capitalist labour extraction crumbled. 'No more métro-boulot-dodo!' grinned Fran. And no more armed guards (just hot police officers), no more weapons, no more invasions and tanks on the streets crushing the protests of 68, or any other year ...

With the immediate halt in mining, the hole in the ozone layer had closed, the polar ice caps had started re-forming, and the weather had become delightful, everywhere. Most people now worked only a couple of hours each day, and their tasks were meaningful and satisfying. They spent the rest of the day in play, rest, and communion with one another. Lots of people read books under trees while formerly endangered birds twittered gently. Others took high-speed, environmentally-friendly trains to visit their friends and family. Fran hummed in anticipation of seeing Charmian when she arrived at the Greek island for the Book Club reunion. As for their other activities, there was no need for slogan painting anymore ... perhaps they'd take up knitting instead.

THE END

Just the further reading and acknowledgements to go! (This is a scholarly work, you know.) Go to page 116.

EPILOGUE

D ing-a-ling!

Normally, Fran loved the cheery sound of the bell above her shoe shop door. It was a friendly companion over the course of her day, merrily punctuating the time she spent chatting with the shoppers of Frankfurt and watching her small business thrive. Ding-a-ling ch-ching!

Even better, sometimes the jovial bell rang as her friends arrived for the weekly Book Club she held out the back of the shop, amongst the shelves of twentieth-century classics and the slogan-painting materials. A bit of book talk, wine drinking, knitting, and rebellious chat was the perfect way to break up the week, if you asked Fran.

Today, though, she barely noticed the bell. Her mind was whirring.

The customer had barely spoken, but with those blue eyes and that dark hair she was the spitting image of her mother — a ghost from the past. Fran had been expecting her, sure, but the sight was still a shock. It wasn't every day you encountered the daughter of a friend you'd said goodbye to decades ago.

Then Fran's nephew, the burly policeman Caspian, had swung by and the two young people had gone off together. Hot on the heels of who knew what at the Frankfurter Buchmesse — something that sounded dangerous, something that sounded political.

Something that sounded a lot like scenes Fran had encountered before.

She'd encountered them with Beatrice's mother Charmian. Ah, the old gang: Fran, Charmian, Sylva and DeNanielle. Fran's eyes misted over. Sitting on the stool behind the counter of her shoe shop, she let her mind travel back, back, back in time, to when they all met. Back to May 68.

To Paris.

The European springtime of history.

The city of love, revolution...and reading.

FURTHER READING
AND
ACKNOWLEDGEMENTS

Congratulations! You have made it to the ACTUAL END!

For further reading about Tante Fran and co, see the other stories by Blaire Squiscoll and associated scholarly work in L'Écrivain (go to page 118).

If you'd like to read more Parisian and May 68 revolutionary works, some of which have been incorporated into and inspired Tante Fran's May 68 Book Club, check out online content for Michèle Bernstein, Simone de Beauvoir and Angela Davis, Guy Debord and the Situationists, Pierre Bourdieu (in particular *Les héritiers*) and the film *Celine and Julie Go Boating*. There are also evocative pictures online of the columns of the Gare du Nord, poster printing, riots and barricades on the streets of Paris in May 68 and, of course, of Victor Noir.

In the creation of the print and digital versions of this text, we would like to thank Will Smith, for securing ISBNS for this book, Simon Rowberry for consultation on online platforms, and an audio guide from *The Guardian* to Paris May 68. We also thank Justine at La Méthode for allowing the distribution of marketing materials, Lautrecs for proof-reading space, and Louisa Preston for expert last-minute cover wrangling.

Funding support from the AHRC Creativity Without Clusters: Overcoming Fragmentation in the Scottish Creative Economy: Creative Economy Postdoctoral Fellowship AH/R013357/1 is gratefully acknowledged.

L'ÉCRIVAIN

Blaire Squiscoll's previous works include *The Frankfurt Kabuff*, an autoethnographic comic erotic thriller set at the Frankfurt Book Fair and featuring some of the characters from *Tante Fran's May 68 Book Club*.

The Frankfurt Kabuff was originally published on Wattpad, then as a print and ebook via Kabuff Books, and in 2023, Wilfrid Laurier University Press published the novella as *The Frankfurt Kabuff Critical Edition*, including the short story 'The Corona Kabuff'.

Other works in the Kabuff-o-World include 'The COP26 Kabuff', available via Blaire's

Wattpad page (https://www.wattpad.com/user/blairesquiscoll). An audiobook edition of *The Frankfurt Kabuff* is rumoured for release. Tante Fran's May 68 Book Club: Choose Your Own Revolution (TFM68BCCYOR) is also available online at https://xwvnw4q6.play.borogove.io/.

When not exploring cupboards and inequalities at book trade events and in critical theory, Blaire enjoys drinking Negronis, ferry journeys, audio tours of Paris, beer spas in Prague, and big-game, off-shore sportfishing trips.

More information on Blaire can be had from https://ullapoolism.wordpress.com/blaire-squiscoll-author/, alongside links to other works from the conceptual school Ullapoolism, co-founded by Beth Driscoll and Claire Squires.

L'ÉDITEUR

Kabuff Books was established in 2018, and is an Ullapoolist make-and-do project. As well as publishing *The Frankfurt Kabuff* (2019) and *Tante Fran's May 68 Book Club* (2025), Kabuff Books partnered with Wilfrid Laurier University Press to co-publish *The Frankfurt Kabuff Critical Edition* (2023), with the assistance of Beth Driscoll and Claire Squires. For more information, see https://ullapoolism.wordpress.com.

THE REAL END

www.ingramcontent.com/pod-product-compliance
Lightning Source LLC
Chambersburg PA
CBHW031056310726
48969CB00007B/2309